A Big Fish Story

JOANNE & DAVID WYLIE

CHILDRENS PRESS Fishy Fish Stories®

JOANNE & DAVID WYLIE

A
BIG
FISH
STORY

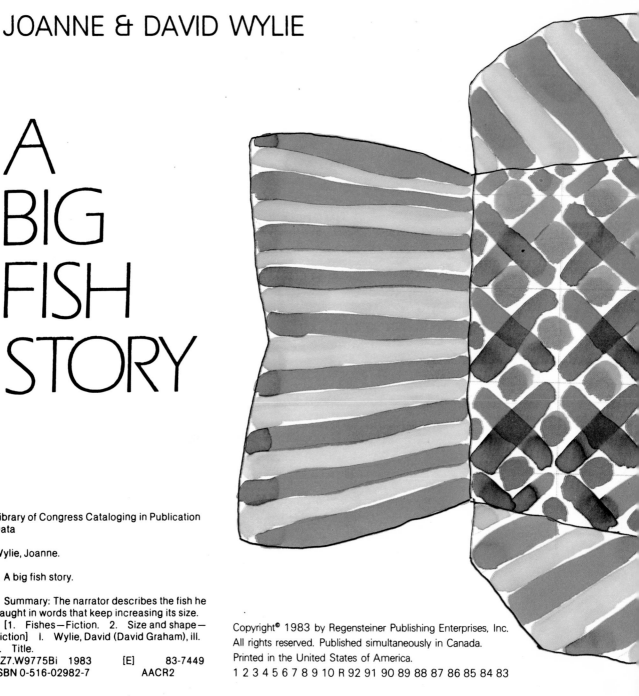

Library of Congress Cataloging in Publication
Data

Wylie, Joanne.

A big fish story.

Summary: The narrator describes the fish he
caught in words that keep increasing its size.
[1. Fishes—Fiction. 2. Size and shape—
Fiction] I. Wylie, David (David Graham), ill.
II. Title.
PZ7.W9775Bi 1983   [E]   83-7449
ISBN 0-516-02982-7   AACR2

Last night I caught a big fish
but I didn't say how big.

My friends asked, "Is it a big fish?"

I said, "Yes, but bigger than big."

"Is it a large fish?"

I said, "Yes, but bigger than large."

"Is it a huge fish?"

I said, "Yes, but bigger than huge."

"Is it a giant fish?"

I said, "Yes, but bigger than giant."

"Is it an enormous fish?"

I said, "Yes, but bigger than enormous."

"Is it an immense fish?"

I said, "Yes, but bigger than immense."

"Is it a tremendous fish?"

I said, "Yes, but bigger than tremendous."

"Is it a mammoth fish?"

I said, "Yes, but bigger than mammoth."

"Is it a gigantic fish?"

I said, "Yes, but bigger than gigantic."

"Can we see it?"

I said, "No, it got away."

Now that's one WHALE of a story.

Do you believe me?

WORD LIST (45 words)

a	is
an	it
asked	large
away	last
believe	mammoth
big	me
bigger	my
but	night
can	no
caught	now
didn't	of
do	one
enormous	said
fish	say
friends	see
giant	story
gigantic	than
got	that's
how	tremendous
huge	we
I	whale
immense	yes
	you

Joanne and David Wylie have collaborated on numerous workbooks, storybooks and learning materials for early childhood.

Joanne, born in Oak Park, Illinois, a graduate of Northwestern University, taught pre kindergarten, kindergarten and first grade for many years. She now devotes her time to writing materials that will help children learn to read and love to read.

David, born in Scotland, attended school in Chicago and studied art at the Art Institute and the F. B. Mizen Academy. He retired early from business and moved to the country to collaborate with his wife Joanne on a series of books for preschool and primary children.

The Fishy Fish Stories

CHILDRENS PRESS ᴘ